Don't Miss Me

Glimpses of God
in photos & poetry

Kim M. Davis

ISBN: 978-1-7327638-4-5 soft cover

Cover and photography by KMD

Lyre & Harp Book Publishing
Monroe, NC 28112
lyreandharp.com

Printed in the United States of America

CONTENTS

Introduction

Glimpses of God can be seen. An eternal love story unfolds when our eyes embrace the sum of photos, poems, and His creation.

In our daily life so much goes unnoticed and unappreciated. We miss the butterflies and flowers and barely hear the birds in the blur of *busyness*. That's the beauty of a camera lens.Through that lens we are made to focus only on the object displayed and its details. We begin to notice the variances of colors, textures, and shades. And if we allow ourselves to sit still long enough, we may even find ourselves wondering *why and how*. And these questions are good, because they indicate that there could possibly be an answer.

And there is an answer.

"Most certainly I tell you, whoever will not receive the Kingdom of God like a little child, he will in no way enter into it. "
Mark 10:15 WEB

Did you know that poetry is defined as an expression of feelings and ideas that move in a certain flow and rhythm?

The Bible contains a lot of poetry. There are whole books dedicated to poems, such as : Psalms, Job, Proverbs, Lamentations, and Song of Solomon. There is also poetic form in much of the Old Testament. And in the New Testament, poetic form can be found in the Beatitudes. Even Jesus spoke in figurative language by use of parables.

This book contains poems that were written during my quiet time with Him. They are meant to be thoughtfully read as you silently reflect on the photo, on yourself, on your situation or circumstance. God promises to help, heal, refresh, and renew, but you must first hear.

Be still, and know that I am God. I will be exalted among the nations. I will be exalted in the earth. Psalm 46:10 WEB

Turn down the noise in your life and turn your attention to Him.

You will find that no two pages are the same. Poetry is from the heart of its creator and is not *cookie-cutter.* Our Great Creator speaks in a language showcasing an array of birds, flowers, trees, seasons, scenery, snowflakes...

He can be described as vivid, magnificent,
awesome, and everlasting, but He will never
be boxed and boring, found only within
a book, program, or pew. So, step out
of tradition and breathe in our immense God.
Allow the Spirits' marvelous movement.
Our Creator is alive and His creation awaits
His coming.

*For we know that the whole creation groans
and travails in pain together until now.*
Romans 8:22 WEB

Photos and poems are just a slight revealing.
A sneak preview into the mighty mystery.
A snippet of the greatest love story :
Gods love for you. An amazing, enduring love
story, with you as a main character.
And instead of a dozen store-bought roses
to proclaim His love, each day He unfolds
His handiwork of sights, smells, sounds,
and colors. The language of God in a living,
love letter.

Will you listen to the birds?
Will you ask the animals?
Will you hear the fish?
Will the earth teach you?

*But ask the animals, now, and they shall
teach you; the birds of the sky, and they shall
tell you. Or speak to the earth, and it shall
teach you. The fish of the sea shall declare
to you. Who doesn't know that in all these,
the hand of the LORD has done this, in
whose hand is the life of every living thing,
and the breath of all humankind?*
Job 12:7-10 NHEB

Or will you continue onward, skimming the
pages of life until you simply find yourself
facing the last chapter?

Will you totally miss Him ?

When the daily cares of life have

twisted you in knots:

Don't miss Me.

When the blanket of darkness begins

to suffocate and enclose:

Don't miss Me.

As your heart shatters from

griefs' heavy hand:

Don't miss Me.

When the comforting breeze refreshes

your hungry skin:

Don't miss Me.

In the newness of the day and in

the crisp early air,

I am there,

waiting.

Don't miss Me.

Don't Miss Me

Glimpses of God
in photos & poetry

***

Kim M. Davis

Following Me is not work. You tire yourself from striving. Do I not provide? Look what I do. I take from your enemies and I give to you. They till the ground and do all of the work but it is you who will eat the crops and hold the riches. And so it is for My children. Let Me do what I will do and they will do what they *believe* they are doing. And all will be well for those who trust in Me.

Don't Miss Me
In Daily Life

The Morning Melody

weaves in my ear
a cheerful reminder that my
loved one is near.

God created the heavens and the earth.

He awakens each day
and guides by His hand
a variety of creatures
in this musical band.

Some warble in splendor
others are quirky in tone
yet a magnificent song
together is sewn.

Then He stitches in light
and with a powerful tug
a display of colors
are knotted and snug.

A masterful scene
held with gold thread
a mysterious wonder
with words He just said.

I gaze at the fabric
as He pins on the time
seasons are fastened
by One so divine.

The skies gleam His glory
the mountains His might
yet I yawn with such tiredness
as He ties up the night

Dwell in His light and sow seeds along your journey.

Even though I walk through the valley of the shadow of death, I will fear no evil, for you are with me. Your rod and your staff, they comfort me. Psalm 23:4 WEB

Living in Christ consists of more than
just a moment of being saved. It is a
journey of intentional intimacy and
learning to listen to His voice. It consists
of terrain depicted by ups and downs.
And contrary to childhood growth, you
do not grow more *independent*, but
instead, you become more *dependent* as
you mature in Him.

In your life journey, you will find yourself
either venturing through the lower valleys
of shadowy, trying times, or moving up
the mountainside to a new destination.
Both require stamina and steadfastness.
Both require a guide.

The Lord is your Shepherd and He will
show you the way. He is your Light.
And in His immense light, death exists
only as a shadow. Remember that
a shadow can loom and cause a chill,
but it is not a reality.

So, give no time to the shadow.
It is only seen when light is nearby.

Christ is your Light and He is always near.

Beloved Butterfly

Butterfly soon to be
you feed,
you die,
you change.
And at the right time
you emerge with wings.
And you fly.
Feeling what you have never
felt before.
Seeing what you have never
seen before.
Experiencing life as never before.
Liberated from your cocoon and
freed from your earthly tether.
Butterfly in the breeze.
Beloved and bejeweled.
Beautifully reborn.

And the LORD went before them by day in a
pillar of a cloud, to lead them the way; and by
night in a pillar of fire, to give them light;
to go by day and night.   Exodus 13:21 KJV

The Light Of His Presence

Do not be distressed.

Each day I am walking ahead and clearing the way. Each day I am walking behind and guarding your back. I do not forget where you are. Do not be fearful and look about. Do not let your heart beat in worry and anxiety. Each day is sustained by Me. So, go ahead; bud and bloom. Nothing is happening that I have not allowed to be so. Each day feel secure in Me and know that

My love for you

moves with you.

And you are always

within my Presence.

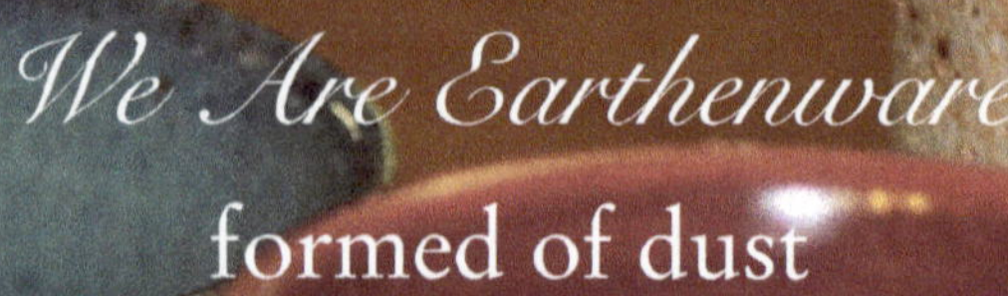

But now LORD, you are our Father, and we are clay, and you are our potter; and we all are the work of your hands. Isaiah 64:8 NHEB

We are similar to pottery. Formed and shaped by Gods hand - no two being exactly the same. Some are irregular in shape, some have been bent by life struggles and pressures, and some stand firm in an array of colors. Each of us are made in Gods image. People may not see the beauty or acknowledge the worth in each piece of clay. They cannot fathom the love that was held and molded between the hands of the Maker nor of the pressure and heat that each finished vessel required, in order to obtain its own look and character. They do not know of the many times that the clay was smashed down and re-formed. All that they see is the finished product on display.

Everyday people pass by the clay artwork. Most barely glance and soon forget each and every masterpiece that was lovingly created. They tend to only draw near to the ones of their liking and to those whose cost is within an acceptable range.

But the Creator, Who held and worked each clay lump through the many seasons of varying pressures, looks on with eyes of love and never forgets the moment of birth, nor of His living breath that forged each one.

Sometimes
You Must Bend

Pride goes before destruction, and a haughty
spirit before a fall. Proverbs 16:18 WEB

The seasons change
and the winds may
blow hard
but I am a tree
standing tall in the yard.

Nothing can move me
nor cause me alarm for
my splendor is great
and naught can do
harm.

Then the wind heard
my detail
and in a gust of might
it shattered my limbs
and laughed in delight.

But Father, I cried,
why this wind did
You send ?

And He told me
politely;
at times you must bend.

See the birds of the sky, they don't sow, neither do they reap, nor gather into barns. Your heavenly Father feeds them. Aren't you of much more value than they? Matthew 6:26 WEB

With my eyes wide open
and my ears tuned to hear,
I take the next step
and your presence is near.

Guiding and leading.

I am unsteady at first
testing if clear, then
I take the next step and
Your presence is near.

Encouraging and enabling.

Like a splash of fresh air
I breathe in - *no fear*
I take the next step
and Your presence is near.

Strengthening and assuring.

My Lord and my Savior
I know and hold dear
that in all of my
movements
Your presence is near.

Loving and lifting.

Do not fear what lies ahead.

I clear the way for you to follow.

Look to Me and you will walk the correct

path. You will not veer off from it.

I love you forevermore and I love those whom

you love. I do not forget My promises and

I do not forget those I love.

Forever are you in My hand.

Forever are you in My heart.

My desire is you.

The birds sing and tell a story that only they

understand. They give songs that lighten;

I give Hope that lasts.

Yesterday. Today. Tomorrow.

Rise and walk, for I Am with you.

Don't Miss Me
In The Struggles & Grief

Many talk about a hole in their heart as
something not good, an infinite emptiness.
A shattered opening that contains only loss
and a memory.

But do you recall the story of Lazarus?
He lay dead inside of a cave, yet when
commanded, he walked out of it alive.
Or how about when weary Elijah hid inside
of a cave and God spoke life to him?
And then there was Jesus, whose lifeless
body lay inside a tomb, *a hole,* and yet He
walked out of it three days later.

Perhaps a hole can appear as a nothingness
yet actually be a doorway for a new
purpose. An entry for new beginnings.

Remember the Apostle Thomas?
He didn't believe that Christ had risen from
the dead. Then he put his finger into the
hole on Jesus' side where Jesus had been
pierced by the soldiers sword. His finger
entered the hole and Thomas believed.

In the ragged, bleak emptiness; life existed.

The Beginning Of New Life

It can be a hole in your heart

Who will believe
and bc drawn to
Christ because
of what your
emptiness
contains?

You Are Not Forgotten

"Are not two sparrows sold for an assarion coin? Not one of them falls on the ground apart from your Father's will. Matthew 10:29 NHEB

With His spoken word

it all came to be.

With outstretched arms

He gave all for me.

Never half-hearted,

the way, yes,

is narrow.

But love not forgotten,

He remembers

the sparrow.

The Eye of The Storm
The place of rest.
May the peace of His presence always calm you
no matter what storms may be blustering about.

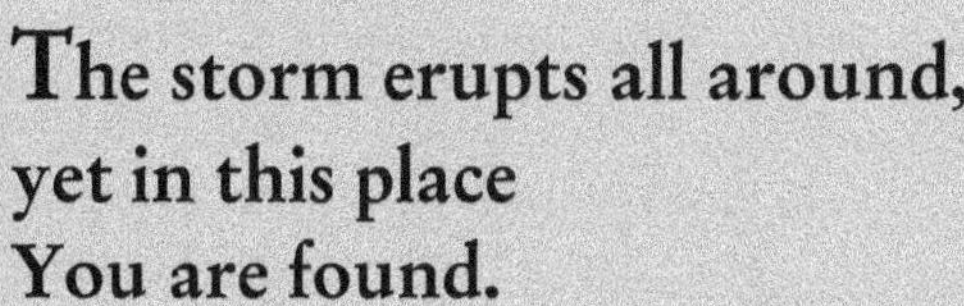

The storm erupts all around,
yet in this place
You are found.

The darkened mass, says to fear,
yet in this place
You are near.

The winds scream and do not cease,
yet in this place,
You are peace.

The clouds emit shards of light,
yet in this place
You are might.

Enveloped in calm, I marvel *why*,
and the answer I realize, is
You are the eye.

*My eyes stay open through
the night watches, that I
might meditate on your word.*
Psalm. 119:148 WEB

He Refreshes

Oh Father today,
as I draw near to You, please
hear my prayer refresh me anew.

Help me to focus
on what lies above
to be as You
and reach out in love.

May I live my life
in such a way,
treasure the moment
and waste not the day.
May my heart be burdened
for who You grieve for,
may I see each face as
never before .

May I let go, so that
in me You live,
and with each blessing I get
I in return give.

May I not grow weary
and yet when I do,
may my faith remain strong
as I cling unto You.

Father today please refresh me anew.

When my life seems purposeless;
He increases my step and prompts
me to lift my head.
When my heart breaks and
shatters to the ground;
He sweeps away the pieces and
reassures me with a new one.
When my eyes water and
my tears flow torrentially
down my face;
He dries them away with
His loving breath and
encourages me to look again.
In a life full of *whens,*
He is my *now*.
There is no end to His goodness.

He Is Your Strength

Lean on Him
when you
begin to sway.

He knows your every sigh and of
the weight that burdens you . He is
ready to send a rain of blessing your
way. If He cares for the flower of
the field , how much more does He
cherish you?

Who
Am I
To Argue

He has said to me, "My grace is sufficient for you, for power is made perfect in weakness." Most gladly therefore I will rather glory in my weaknesses, that the power of Christ may rest on me. 2 Corinthians 12:9 NHEB

When pressures push me away,
His word pulls me near.
When loneliness engulfs me,
He encircles me with His presence.
When thoughts threaten to take me,
His hand secures me,
and I am anchored by His touch.

If I say that I am a nobody,
He declares to me that I am precious.
If I remind Him of my past failures,
He says there is no condemnation in Him.
If I stammer out my weaknesses
He speaks of His abiding strength.

For all that I think I am
He insists that He is always more.

Who am I to argue?
I am who He declares me to be, and
I am complete in Him.

A flower within the refuge of a mighty oak.

Ask What I Have
Determined For You
Also delight yourself in the LORD,
and he will give you the desires
of your heart Psalm 37:4 NHEB

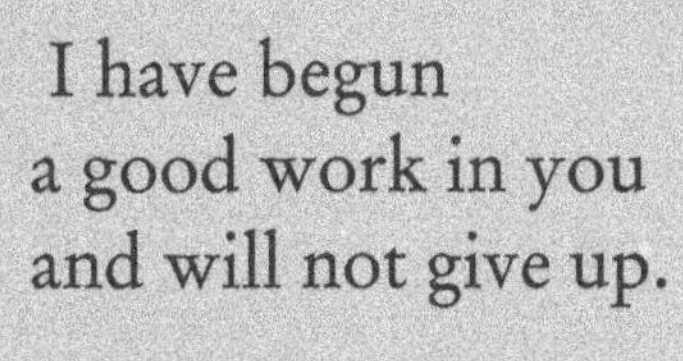

I have begun
a good work in you
and will not give up.

I am the Beginning
and the End of everything.

You study the sun and
you measure the rain,
but the heat and
harvests are Mine.

I direct the sun.
I release the rain.

There is no need to look
about and fret over the
abundance or lack.

Look only to Me.
Ask that you may
receive.

In Him
You Are Healed

Sorrow, pain, heartache, and death.
We all walk the same valley.

And God shall wipe away all tears from their eyes; and there shall be no more death, neither sorrow, nor crying, neither shall there be any more pain; for the former things are passed away. Revelation 21:4 KJV

I walked the road
I've trod before.
Pain and sorrow,
a festering sore.

My thoughts so heavy
in heartfelt cry,
I lifted my eyes
to the heavenly skies.

*　　*　　*

Soon birds I heard
among the gloom.
My eyes even witnessed
a flower in bloom.

Then a voice above
said, "child you're sealed."

"There is no sore,
you've always been healed."

At times I am a little whisper that lingers in your ear or a fierce storm that shakes your world. Perhaps a nudge that prompts you into action. Maybe even a thought that you just cannot shake or an urgency that cannot be ignored.

I am the song that springs from your soul and the melody that moves the psalmist. I settle on you like a dove and ignite upon you in flames.

I am the One from the beginning who hovered over the waters and I am the water that has cleansed you. I am He who washes away the sin and He who brings new life out from the flood waters.

Don't Miss Me
In The Comforting Breeze

When he had said this, he breathed on them,
and said to them, 'Receive the Holy Spirit.'
John 20:22 WEB

Do you realize that Jesus did not do any
miracles or heal anyone until after He
had been baptized and the Spirit as a dove
rested upon Him? It is the Holy Spirit that
gives life and He was there hovering over
the deep waters at the beginning of creation.
He is also given to each believer to help
and empower them.

You cannot see the Spirit move and you
cannot touch Him, but you can detect His
presence. For just as the wind itself
is unseen, you can still know where it is by
observing the movement in the leaves,
grasses, and trees. What you see is the
effect that the wind is having on all that it
touches. You can also see what the Holy
Spirit is effecting and touching. You can
discern this by looking for the movement
that is caused by Him.

*Have you noticed the swaying of the one
who is seeking something, leaning towards God?*

*Are you alert to the rustling of the one whose questions
indicate a thirst?*

Perhaps you are a witness to the Spirits movement.

Watching the clouds as they
drift through the sky,
I wondered the impossible
and thought to question why.

Can you touch the clouds?
A voice inside me asked;
and my answer came out quickly,
they are outside my grasp.

You are looking and seeing
with only your eyes,
a voice chided me gently,
it took me by surprise.

Well, I am too short
and they are too high:
How could it be possible,
I replied with a sigh.

Stop looking at things through a natural approach.
Ask Him to bring to you, whatever is out of your reach.

Yet, my gaze lingered upward
far above my head,
but stature and distance
kept my thinking dead.

But you don't need height
a whisper came to me,
for all is within reach
when you're holding the key.

So, I thought even deeper,
and finally I knew.
Then His tender voice breathed,

Let Me

bring them

down to you.

Perhaps His help is closer than we realize.
Do you recall the servant Haggai? She was sent away into the wilderness with her son. Crying in misery and faint from thirst, the Angel of the Lord revealed a well of water to her. She and her son drank from it. Gods word says that the well was revealed. Not that it just magically appeared.
It was already there, but not seen. Refreshing relief was so close, but she may have missed it, if she had not cried out to Him. Don't miss all that He has for you. Your refreshment, your desire, may be closer than you know.

There's a song in my heart.
There's a song in my soul.
And it praises my Lord,
rises up from below.

There's a song in my heart
it sings of the truth
it tells of the Lamb
and His deep love for you.

Oh, Oh, Oh,
would you sing this
with me?

He listens for you
like the birds of the tree.

Sing to Him.
Reach for Love.
Sing to our King
enter His kingdom above.

*LORD, in the morning you
shall hear my voice.*
Psalm 5:3 NHEB

His Spirit
Travels

The
Trees

And the birds on the
dew drops are
singing, a song that
reaches my ear.
In the whispering
wind He is calling;
Come to Me, my
beloved, and hear.

And the flowers
dance into the
dawning
And the breeze
caresses my skin.
Come to Me my
beloved I am longing,
don't miss Me this
morning again.

Safe in His love I surrender.
Sealed in His kiss I am free.
Safe in His love I surrender.
My God, my Father, and me.

And the joy of the new day is lifting.
His grace is pulling me near.
In the soft curtain of sunlight,
He wraps me in arms of no fear.

Safe in His love I surrender.
Sealed in His kiss I am free.
Safe in His love I surrender.
My Lord, my Savior, and me.

Come to Me my child - I am waiting.
Come to Me and simply just be.
Take My hand and reach for
tomorrow, as My Spirit travels the
trees.

Safe in His love I surrender.
Sealed in His kiss I am free.
Safe in His love I surrender.
My Friend, my Beloved, and me.

The Spirit and the bride say, "Come!"
He who hears, let him say, "Come."
He who is thirsty, let him come. He
who desires, let him take the water of
life freely. Revelation 22:17 NHEB

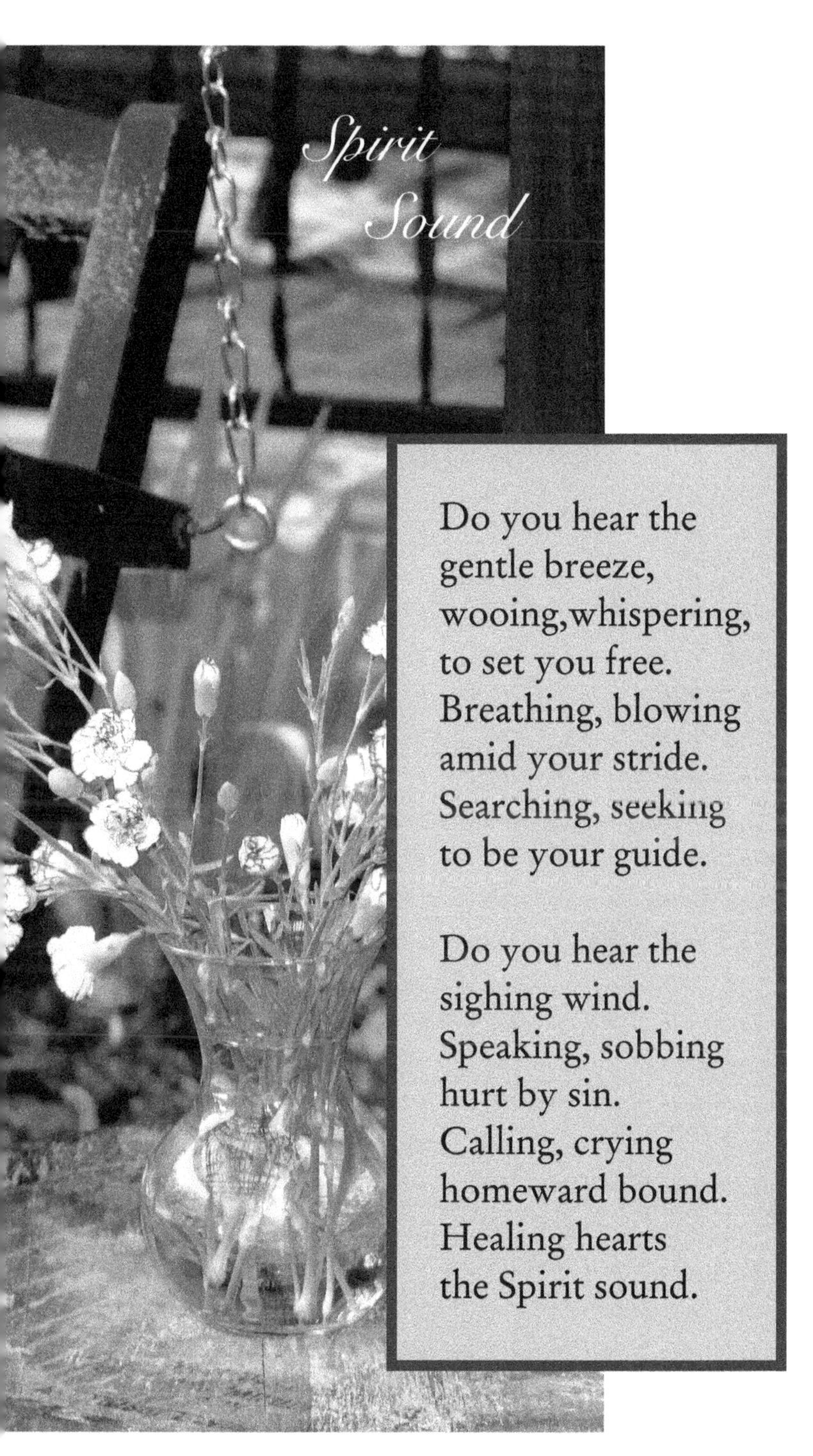
Spirit
Sound

Do you hear the
gentle breeze,
wooing,whispering,
to set you free.
Breathing, blowing
amid your stride.
Searching, seeking
to be your guide.

Do you hear the
sighing wind.
Speaking, sobbing
hurt by sin.
Calling, crying
homeward bound.
Healing hearts
the Spirit sound.

In the olive grove ,
did you hear Him pray?
He knows your name.
Has the stone rolled away?

A heartfelt cry
for you - He said,
and in return
His blood ran red.

He claimed your sins
the curse, the tree,
insults and scorn
to set you free.

The nails bore His weight
as He hung there that day:
Consider the cost.
Has the stone rolled away?

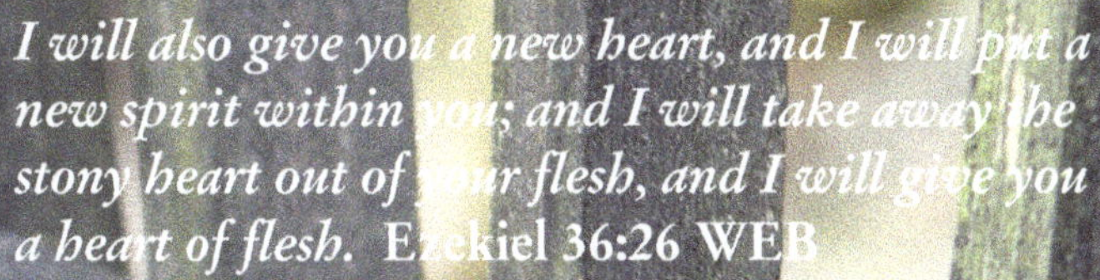

Below His feet
they fought for His clothes.
A crown of thorns
encircled the rose.

In anguish He breathed
and they heard Him say;
Father forgive them.
Has the stone rolled away?

He carried your sins
to the chiseled out tomb.
The victor of death
gave life in full bloom.

Pieces of cloth
where once He did lay.
Mary rejoiced -
The stone rolled away!

Prepare for the journey.

Wisdom leads the procession and righteousness is the way. Let My Word move you. Hide it deep within, for it is your source, your refreshment, and your Guide.

Guard your heart, for it acts as your compass. Never carry baggage, for it will only be a weighty burden and hinder your stride.

And remember to thoughtfully consider each day, season, and the time that I have given.

For I long to gather you near and whisper *well done; now enter your rest.*

Don't Miss Me
In The New Day

The Journey

I called to the Lord
and He answered.
I cried to the Lord
and He heard.

Come, He said.
*Leave your worries
and let Me live.*

Come, He called.
*Forget your cares
and find Me.*

I reached for my God
and He moved.

Closer He came.

Nearer I went.

And we became one.

As the brief gusts lift the evergreen
needles; Your breath lifts me.
It moves me. It stirs me and causes
me to be content wherever I am placed
and to rest assuredly on that which
I cannot see.

Refreshed

Wave after wave:
I re-work the
shoreline.
Gently softening
the rough edges.
Filling in the
abandoned
holes
dug by others, and
carrying away the
telltale signs of
brokenness and
incompleteness.
Wave after wave:
I quench your
dryness
and
remove the
footprints
of those
who
have walked
on you.

Wave after wave:
I wash away the
worldly debris
that attempts
to
cling
to you.
Wave after wave:
My hand is
always
upon you.
At times
you are
completely
immersed.
Soaking
in
Me.

Renewed

And at other
times
I release you in
newness.
Glistening in
firmness.
Wave after wave:
I re-work the
shoreline.
The place where
you
and I
meet.
The place
exposed
to
My
touch.

Wave after wave:
I give and
I take
away.
Wave after wave:
you are
replenished,
refreshed,
reshaped and
renewed.

Day
by
day.

Have you ever discovered that praying can be so difficult?

Psalm 100 instructs us to enter His gates with thanksgiving and His courts with praise. Do you realize that when you pray to God that you are entering His dwelling place? Have you ever thought about how you approach His throne? Are you entering humbly, truthfully, and in full acknowledgment of who He is and of how privileged you are to come before Him. You are given access to Him, through your High Priest and Savior, Christ Jesus.

Does He answer prayer? Yes, He does. Many times though, the answer is not immediate. Prayer encompasses and impacts many other people, in ways that only He understands. Remember that His timing is different than yours and that there is spiritual warfare always about you. Spiritual attack is heavy whenever you go to Him in prayer. Satan does not want you in prayer and he will use tactics to discourage and undermine your fellowship with Father.

Did you know that Daniel prayed and fasted for three weeks before his answer came from God? Daniels answer came on the 21st day of prayer, yet the angel was sent immediately when Daniel prayed. The book of Daniel tells us that the angel was held up in a spiritual battle before getting to Daniel.

So, cry out your heart to Him and never cease in prayer. Give God all of your pieces. Be devoted like Daniel.

A time exists when your answer breaks out of the spiritual realm and enters the natural realm.

Prayer is important because it starts putting everything into position - yourself included.

What Could Prayer Do

with all this brokenness ?

Quit looking at the whole scene and begin moving in the thick of it.

Trust in the LORD
with all your heart,
and do not
lean on your own
understanding.
In all your ways
acknowledge him,
and he will make
your paths straight.
Proverbs 3:5-6 NHEB

Teasing The Sky

A Squirrel Thought

I watched a squirrel
as he sailed by,
branch to branch he teased the sky.

A maze of brambles,
twisted so thick,
I marveled at how he could jump so quick.

Awaiting his fall
so sure of his plight,
he tapped a frail twig but continued in flight.

Maneuvering and moving
he went on his way,
one jump at a time he didn't delay.

What looked impossible
from my point of view,
was a visible path that only he knew.

Yet, I couldn't see it
and the reason why,
is because I hesitate, to tease the sky.

Victory Follows
The Obstacle

It is I , do not be afraid.

It is I who moves you into the battle
and it is I who clears the battleground.

It is I who leads you into the wilderness
and it is I who provides the path to follow.

It is I who guides you into the sea
and it is I who opens the watery corridor.

It is I who does all of this.

Do not falter when you see what lies
ahead.

Keep looking to Me.
Keep moving in Me.

For it is I - Do not be afraid.

Bear one another's burdens, and so you will fulfill the law of Christ.   Galatians 6:2 NHEB
Gather The Treasures
Pray for them.

I gather the treasures
He leads me to find
seeking and searching
forever in mind.

With painful tears
I cry as I hold,
the beautiful glimmers
of worth yet untold.

Bound to my heart
these gems made of clay
I raise them to Him
to give them away.

In love I may linger
caressing the load,
but the weight is too heavy
and long is the road.

I then pray them to Him,
how precious they are
and He opens up heaven
accepting my jar.

I quicken my pace,
for empty once more,
this race is not over
there's more yet to store.

The righteous shall flourish like the palm tree. He will grow like a cedar in Lebanon. They are planted in the LORD'S house. They will flourish in our God's courts. They will still bring forth fruit in old age. Psalm 92:12-14 NHEB

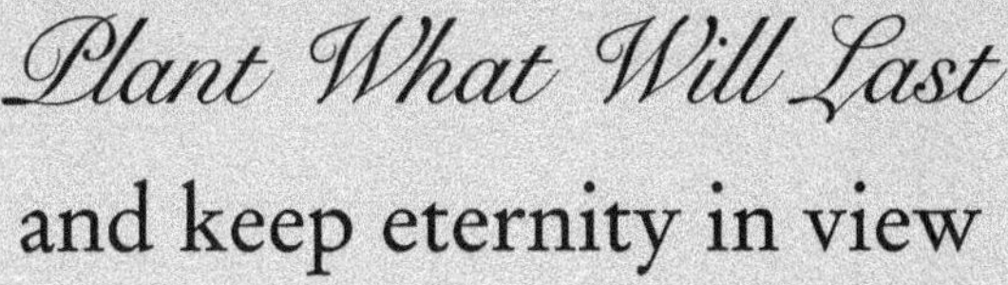

Plant What Will Last

and keep eternity in view

I stand in your midst
yet is it me you see?
I am typically found near
the decaying debris.

I was planted by God
and bear the heat of the day.
I will be here for ages
when you've long passed away.

I provide shelter for many
I protect and I keep.
Yet you miss my significance
as you lie down to sleep.

I can tell you such mysteries
of things you don't know.
Yet all bear the lesson:
You reap what you sow.

I opened a letter
jasmine scent drifted by
breathing in deeply
was my sudden reply.

In the very first sentence
as onward I read
the soft bud of a rose
was what that line said.

In thought I did linger
considering the mail
and on the next page
was the smallest of snail.

Gods
Love
Letter

White flowers so fragrant
with face lifted high
flowed from the long limbs
and framed the blue sky.

Words written in nature
so easy, yet bold,
with each stroke of His hand
a story was told.

In awe of His glory,
signed on the last line, was
"With love forever,
You'll always be Mine."

*Thank you Holy Father for the beauty
You create and sustain each day !*

Walking With Jesus

For a few steps and a few moments, the Apostle Peter defied the laws of this earth as he walked on the water toward Jesus.

He said, "Come." Peter stepped down from the boat, and walked on the water and went toward Jesus. But when he saw the strong wind, he was afraid, and beginning to sink, he yelled, saying, "Lord, save me." Matthew 14:29-30 NHEB

And what about you? Do you come to the Living Water and drink deeply: Stepping out each day in fullness of faith and Spirit? Have you dared to leave the boat of safety?

Perhaps, if we would follow His voice and embrace the way of the water, we may miss the many stones that cause us to stumble.

The Gritty Sand

One day, as Jesus and I were walking along the sandy shoreline, the wet sand began to stick between my toes. I told Jesus that the gritty feeling was kind of bothersome. Jesus looked at me sincerely and asked, "what do you do?"Well, I replied, I have to brush it away as it gets kind of irritating. Sometimes, though, if I walk a lot, it will just dry out and fall away."

     For the life of me, I don't know why we weren't talking about the seashells or the bright sunlight. Why there was no comment about the puffy clouds casually coasting above. It just seemed kind of odd to be talking with Jesus about the wet sand. Yet, it was such a gorgeous day and He seemed genuinely intrigued with me and my answers. And then He calmly asked me: "Do you think life is gritty?"And I paused. In a quick moment I thought of the times of deep hurt, the times of feeling alone, the times of intense struggles, and I knew that He already knew, so I said, "Yes, Father, I find that life can be really gritty." "So, what do you do?" He gently questioned. With a half hearted smile and slight shrug I replied, "I try to brush it away."

     Once again I was struck by our odd conversation. I watched the waves gently rolling. I so enjoyed just being with Him.

"Do you know what I do?" He continued.
"I put my foot into the water and the grit goes
away. My foot gets wet. Have you tried that?"
"Well, yes, I have at times, but it just gets all
gritty again when my foot touches the sand."
     Then Jesus looked at me intently. And in that
moment I could see His love and patience.
I understood the beauty of the day and knew
that it all was wrapped up in Him. Then He said
so simply, "it gets gritty again because you keep
getting out. You must learn to stay in the
water." And in that instant, my chest became
heavy and I knew what He meant. Far too many
times when the swells have threatened, I have
taken my eyes off of Him. Way too often
as the waves of life pushed me down, I have
tried to walk in my own strength.
Far too many times and way too often I have
trudged with extra weight beneath my feet, until
it dried and crumbled away. Far too many times
and way too often, I have walked in my
strength and not that of the Spirit.
     Not in the water, not on the water, but on my
own. My heart broke in realization and tears
flooded my eyes. I began to cry at my failure.
"Don't cry," Jesus' soft voice reassured.
"It's just a lesson."
"It was hard for Peter to walk on the water too."

May you walk boldly by faith, empowered in the Spirit.

May you never miss a moment immersed in His presence.

Father God,

You are immense and thought provoking,
delicate and graceful,
awe-inspiring and enveloping.
Bigger than I can imagine.
You are the Beginning and the End
of everything that I even know
or understand.
Who am I?
A bit of dust formed and fashioned
by Your breath.
I am small when standing
and inadequate in Your presence.
Yet You have chosen me .
And Your Word assures me
that I am Your special one
occupying that special place
in Your heart.
I don't understand it all,
but I choose to honor the One
who gives it all.
Thank You Father for keeping me so close.
I am in awe of You.

My Testimony

I was once asked by my pastor, *why am I on fire for God?* The following begins my answer and is what I told the congregation.

I am on fire for God because I reached a point where I realized that God had been working in my life orchestrating circumstances.
I reached a place where I became *aware* of His presence. And it was at a place of emptiness, that I gained my sight.

On Feb 17, 2011, I received news that my first cousin had died. (He was on my dads side of the family). I bought some wind chimes as a bereavement gift and began packing them to send to my aunt who lived out of state.
As I was boxing them up, my son Landon came into the kitchen and sat at the table.
I explained what I was doing and related to him who had died. Three days later, Feb 20, 2011, I received news that my first cousin died. (He was on my moms side of the family).
Once again, I bought a set of wind chimes. And once again I was explaining this death to Landon as he sat at the kitchen table watching me box them up to send to my uncle who lived out of state. Nine days later, March 1, 2011, Landon was pronounced dead.

I had known the death of my mom, friends,
and of acquaintances, but my sons death
delivered things I had never known - The things
he would never know. He would never have
a fiance, a wedding, be best-man in his brothers
weddings, nor have children and a family
of his own. His death resonated loudly; *the end.*

During the time that I waited on family to arrive
for the funeral, I did a lot of soul searching.
I cried to God and said, *I know You are there.*
There has got to be something more than this.
Then I threw in the towel to this life and
declared, *I'm all in.*
What do You want me to do?

The words of this scripture became my song:

Don't be afraid, for I am with you.
Don't be discouraged, for I am your God.
I will strengthen you and help you.
I will hold you up with my victorious
right hand.   Isaiah 41:10 NLT

My chimes, sent to me from my sister, arrived
shortly after the funeral.

Why Am I On Fire For God?

My Personal Glimpse Of God

On the same day that Kim and Mike struggled through the funeral service of their 23 year old twin son, a stray, sick beagle showed up at their home. Heartbroken and grieving for their son, they gave the stray dog some food and provided a blanket for him to lay upon. Two days later, still not knowing what to do with the stray dog (for they already owned two dogs) Kim called and was able to get a same day veterinarian appointment.

As Kim sat inside the empty waiting room, with the beagle sitting on the floor next to her, an unknown woman came from the back exam area carrying her small terrier on her shoulder. Kim noticed that the woman with long hair and glasses kept looking at her and the beagle, when finally the lady said,"beagles are good dogs." Not feeling like talking, but responding out of politeness, Kim replied, "I guess so, this one is a stray." The unknown lady then said, "I had a beagle show up one time, and I did the same thing you are doing. I took him to the vet to get treatment, but even though my mom told me that it was a *sign* and I should keep the beagle, I had to give him away. This one, she continued, indicating the yorkie terrier on her shoulder, would not allow it. So, I gave the stray to a man living in the countryside."

Intrigued by her phrase that, *it was a sign*, Kim related to the lady that the beagle, sitting next to her, showed up the same day as her sons funeral. The lady with long hair and glasses began to cry as she looked at Kim and said, "my son also died. He would have been 23 years old this year." In disbelief, Kim replied, "my son was 23 years old when he died." In the still empty lobby, the unknown lady stepped towards Kim, leaned over, hugged her and sobbingly said, "God bless you, it is still so hard for me." Without thought Kim hugged her back, as the amazed receptionist who heard the story stared on. As if comparing notes, the lady then said that her son was born December 2nd and Kim said that her son was born December 10th. The lady then told Kim her sons name and asked Kim the name of her son. Kim answered, "my sons name was Landon." Tears once again welled up in her eyes as she stared unbelievingly. She related that her son had loved this one movie so much, *A Walk To Remember,* and that he would watch it over and over again. The leading person in that movie, was named Landon."

I never did learn her name. The astonished receptionist, the only person that heard our conversation, kept saying that God works in mysterious ways.

With time and a deeper relationship, I have come to understand that God does work in ways that are far beyond my comprehension. Even when I feel alone and think that He has forgotten and is silent, Father God is watching and working.

And there is something else I have realized: *There are no coincidences in the life of the believer.*

On May 5, 2017, six years after my sons death, through a bizarre set of events involving my oldest son, I now know the lady who offered this stranger a hug. We both learned that she had actually met and talked with Landon on his birthday, just prior to his death. And not only that, but that I have spoken with her for several years, via telephone, scheduling appointments.

So, to answer the question: *Why am I on fire for God?*

Because my mysterious God, my loving Father, is on fire for me !

We tell the stories of Jonah and the whale,
of the ark that Noah built and the many pairs
of animals. We marvel at how so many could
fit inside the ark. We wonder at how Jonah
stayed three days and nights inside the whale.
But we mostly miss this: How was the whale
at the right place, at the right time, when Jonah
went over-board the ship? How did the
animals know when to journey to the ark
or where the ark was located?
Who told them?

May this book be a blessing to you and may
my testimony serve to strengthen you.
And if you can hear His voice, then answer;
then speak. For that is your reasonable
service.

The Spirit and the bride say, "Come!"
He who hears, let him say, "Come."
Revelation 22:17 NHEB

So, yes, "come."

Barney
March 7 2011 - February 18 2021

Thank you Father for the obedient heart
of a beloved beagle, (Barney) who heard
Your voice and went.

Something we should all seek to do.

www.ingramcontent.com/pod-product-compliance
Lightning Source LLC
Chambersburg PA
CBHW040931050726
47507CB00022B/336